A Perfect Pork Stew

by Paul Brett Johnson

ORCHARD BOOKS   NEW YORK

Orchard Books, 95 Madison Avenue, New York, NY 10016

Manufactured in the United States of America
Printed by Barton Press, Inc. Bound by Horowitz/Rae
Book design by Mina Greenstein

The text of this book is set in 14 pt. Meridien Medium.
The illustrations are colored pencil and watercolor reproduced in full color.
10   9   8   7   6   5   4   3   2   1

Library of Congress Cataloging-in-Publication Data
Johnson, Paul Brett.
A perfect pork stew/ by Paul Brett Johnson.   p.   cm.
Summary: When Ivan the Fool meets Baba Yaga, the witch of Russian
folklore fame, on a day that has begun badly for her, he outwits her
by making dirt soup, getting a fine, fat pig in the bargain.
ISBN 0-531-30070-6. — ISBN 0-531-33070-2 (lib. bdg.)
[1. Witches—Fiction.   2. Characters in literature—Fiction.]
I. Title.   PZ7.J6354Pf   1998   [Fic]—dc21   97-21962

AUTHOR'S NOTE

Growing up in Appalachia, I have heard my share of folktales. Perhaps that has something to do with how this story came about.

A few years ago I took a trip to Russia. I wandered awestruck along the canals of St. Petersburg and beneath the gilded domes of Moscow. Everywhere I turned I saw evidence of an incredibly rich folk heritage. I left wanting to illustrate a tale from that fascinating part of the world.

But the stories I liked best had, it seemed, already been published time and again. What was there to do except concoct my own tale? I started with a couple of stock characters from Russian lore. I added a pinch of tall tale, a bit of swapping motif, and a good dose of the sillies. It wasn't long before *A Perfect Pork Stew* began to bubble.

—*Paul Brett Johnson*

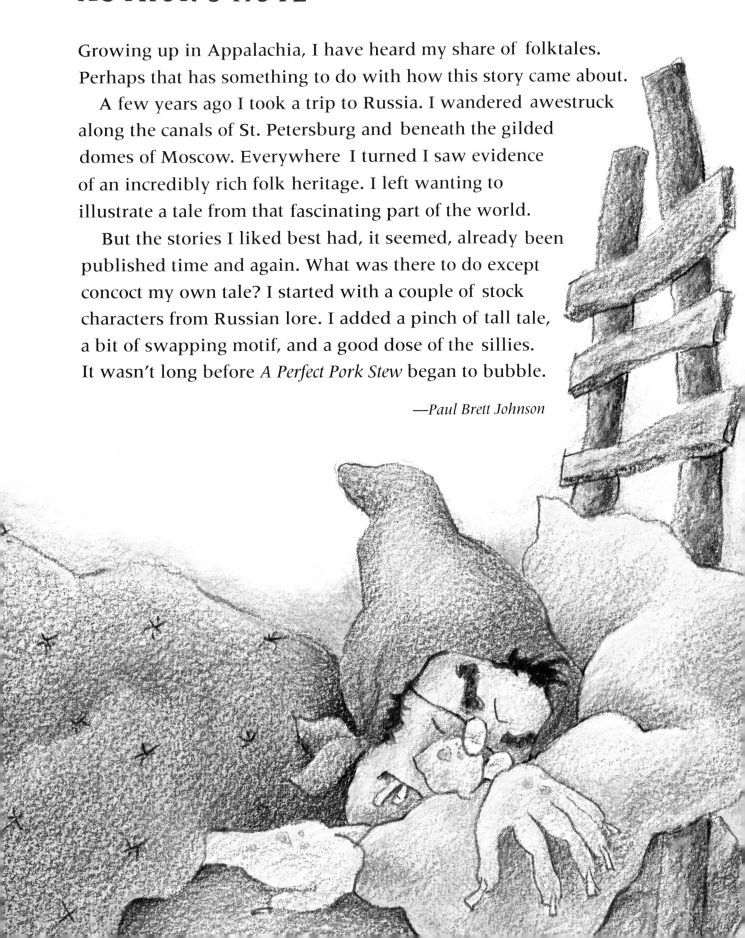

One gray Russian morning
old Baba Yaga got up on the
wrong side of the bed—
something a witch ought never do!

"Oh, bat brains!" Baba Yaga grumbled. "It's sure to be a bad day."

And so it was.

First of all, she burned the breakfast critter.

Then she spilled an entire vial of snake venom.

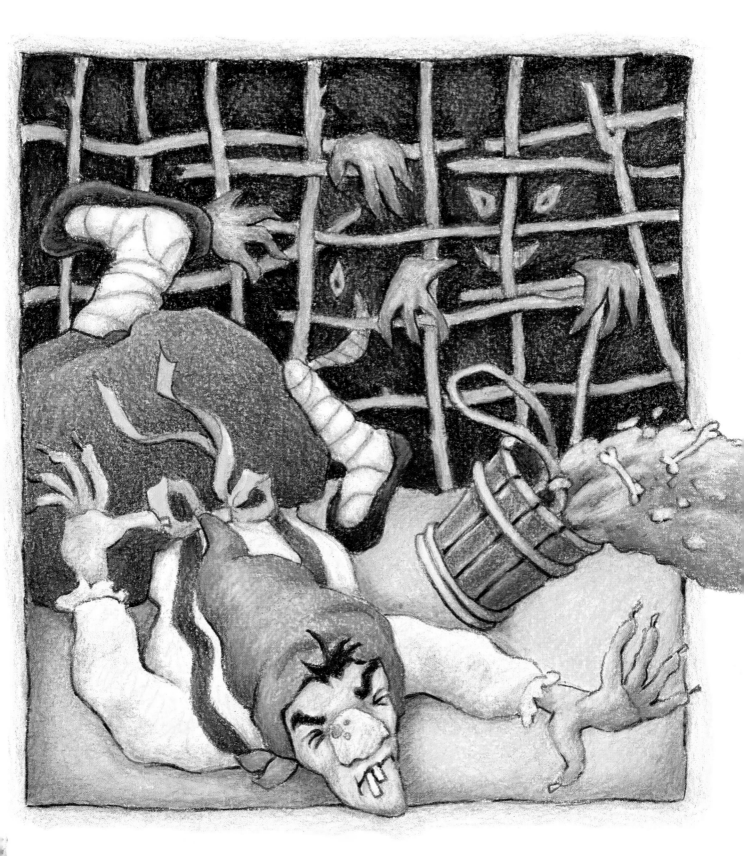

But the worst thing happened when Baba Yaga went out
to feed the goblins. She tripped and fell and broke
her spectacles.

She tried to mend them, but without her spectacles she couldn't make out the directions in her hex-it-yourself book.

So when she heard someone coming along the road, she strained her eyes and wrinkled her blue, warty nose. "Who goes there? Speak up or I'll turn you into a thorny-headed newt!" she screeched.

"It's only Ivan," answered a young lad who was pushing a wheelbarrow filled with dirt clods.

"Ivan the Fool?"

"So some call me," said Ivan.

The witch squinted at Ivan's barrow. To her weak eyes, it appeared to contain a sweet pink pig.

"Ah. Well, Ivan the Fool, what do you intend doing with that pig in your barrow?"

Ivan looked at his barrow. What pig? he thought. I may be a fool, but I'm not stupid. That old granny is up to something, and if I know what's good for me, I had better play along.

"Well, babushka, I'm off to market," said he. "This big, fat, juicy pig is sure to fetch a pouch full of rubles."

Baba Yaga drooled. She thought, This simpleton is an easy mark. I'll have myself a pork dinner before today is done.

"Don't bother going to market, dearie," she crooned. "I'll make you a better trade. Just build a nice fire under my cook pot and drop in that pig. I'll give you one of my very best magical spells."

"Hmmm . . ." The lad thought it over. "Exactly which spell?"

"I shall turn your evil stepmother into a toad."

"I don't have a stepmother," said Ivan.

"Then I'll conjure up a demon to settle your scores."

"I bear no grudges and I have no scores to settle," said Ivan.

"You drive a hard bargain, fool. But certainly you'll swap a mere pig for this magic turnip, else you be a fool indeed."

"Magic turnip?"

"Just drop it in a pot with a little cabbage and a few onions and you'll never scrape bottom—soup enough to feed the whole family for the Czar knows how long."

Ivan figured his mother could surely use such an amazing turnip. "The deal is done!" he said. So he built a roaring fire under the cook pot and dumped in the entire load of dirt clods along with a bucket of water.

The lad tossed his turnip into the wheelbarrow and started on his way. "I can't believe that old hag bought my load of dirt clods for a magic turnip," Ivan said, smirking.

Baba Yaga stirred her cook pot. "Hee, hee! I can't believe that stupid bumpkin fell for the magic turnip ruse," she cackled.

The witch sniffed. She took a taste to see how her stew was coming along. "FFFWUUUP!" she spat. "Hold it right there, Ivan the Fool! This is the vilest stuff I have ever tasted. I've a good mind to turn you into a stump-tailed shrew."

In his life, Ivan had wished to be many things, but never a stump-tailed shrew. He quickly decided to try and outsmart the witch.

"Perhaps it needs a little something else," said the lad. He pretended to taste the stew. He thought a moment. "Well, it could certainly use a turnip," he said.

"You have my only turnip," said the witch. "Give it back and we'll put it in the stew."

"But this is a magic turnip. You said so yourself. I'm taking it to my mother."

"I have something far better than a magic turnip. Here is a thinking cabbage head. It will answer all your questions," said Baba Yaga. "Now, fool, drop the turnip into the stew, and the thinking cabbage head is yours."

Ivan figured his father could surely use such an amazing cabbage head. "The deal is done," he said, and he dropped the turnip into the cook pot.

The lad tossed his cabbage into the wheelbarrow and started on his way. I can't believe that old granny bought my turnip for a thinking cabbage head, thought Ivan, very pleased with himself.

Baba Yaga stirred her cook pot. "Hee, hee," she chuckled. "I can't believe that dimwit fell for the thinking-cabbage-head trick." She sniffed and took a taste to see how her stew was coming along.

"ARRRRGH!" the witch choked. "Don't take another step, Ivan the Fool, else I'll turn you into a flap-legged lizard! This has to be the worst pork stew ever."

Since Ivan did not care to become a flap-legged lizard, he pretended to taste the stew. "Hmmm. Better. But it could surely use some cabbage."

"Cabbage? I just gave you my only cabbage. You best drop it in the pot."

"But you said it was a thinking cabbage head. I'm taking it to my father."

"Fool, fool, fool! Why would you want a mere cabbage when I have a wondrous wonder to offer. Here, take these onions instead. They will make all the young ladies cry for you. In no time at all, you'll find a wife."

Ivan figured his brother, who was very much in love, could surely do with such amazing onions. "Very well. I'll trade."

Ivan put the cabbage into the cook pot, took his onions, and started on his way. For a witch, that old bag of bones is not very smart, thought Ivan. I can't believe she bought my cabbage head for such wondrous onions.

What a pea-brain! thought Baba Yaga as she tended her stew. She sniffed and stirred and tasted.

"BLECCCH! Your days as a boy are getting fewer," she shouted at Ivan. "Do something with this horrid concoction or I'll turn you into a slick-bellied sea slug!"

Ivan pretended to taste the stew. "Well, it's certainly coming along. But a few onions would help a lot."

"I have no onions. You have my onions. Put the onions in the stew."

"But these onions will make all the young ladies cry. I am taking them to my brother."

The old witch turned fiery red. "Ivan the Fool, it's been a bad day, and you're not helping matters. Now drop in those onions BEFORE I LOSE MY TEMPER!"

Ivan trembled all the way down to his toenails. He did as the witch instructed.

Ivan pretended to taste the stew. "Uhmmmm. Much better," he said. "All it needs now is a dash of paprika."

"Paprika? PAPRIKA?" cried Baba Yaga. "Ground bat wings I have. Spiderwort I have. Wolfsbane I have. Paprika I do not have."

"I would gladly go to market for paprika, if only I had some money," offered Ivan.

"There's money in the snake-eye jar. Take what you need and not a ruble more. And be quick about it. I'm starving."

Ivan took a handful of coins. He feared paprika might be
expensive, so he took another handful.

As it turned out, paprika was not expensive at all. Ivan had enough money to buy a fat pig as well. This fine pig should make that old witch happy, he thought.

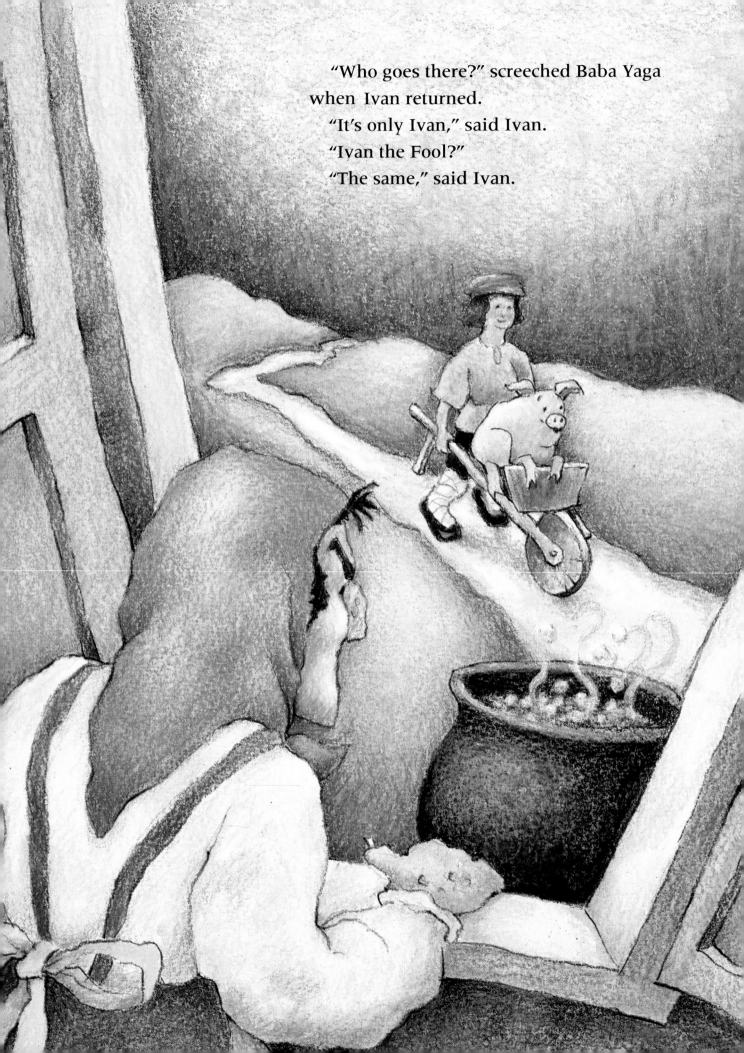

"Who goes there?" screeched Baba Yaga when Ivan returned.

"It's only Ivan," said Ivan.

"Ivan the Fool?"

"The same," said Ivan.

Baba Yaga looked at the pig in Ivan's barrow. To her weak, watery eyes it appeared to be a load of dirt clods.

"What do you intend doing with that barrow full of dirt clods?" asked Baba Yaga.

Ivan looked at his barrow. What dirt clods? he thought. I may be a fool, but I'm not stupid. That old granny is up to something, and if I know what's good for me, I had better play along.

"Well, babushka, I'm off to chink the chimney."

"You earn your name, fool. You must have good clay to chink a chimney. Now see if you can doctor up this stew. Else I'll turn you into a hairy-crested cockroach!"

So Ivan emptied the sack of paprika into the cook pot. He pretended to sip a spoonful. "Uhmm, uhmm, uhmm. Now there's a perfect pork stew," he bragged. "That's the best pork stew I have ever tasted."

"Here. Let me taste." Baba Yaga grabbed the spoon. She made little smacking noises. "I've had better," she said. But by now, the witch was so hungry she decided to eat a bowl full anyway.

"Now be gone, Ivan the Fool, before I think of something really dreadful to turn you into."

So Ivan took his wheelbarrow and the pig and happily went on his way.

That night, Baba Yaga developed an awful stomachache.
She thought her belches smelled a bit like a damp dirt cellar.
The witch squinted and fumbled her way to bed,
reminding herself to get a new pair of spectacles tomorrow.
Then she crawled in—on the wrong side.

And that is something a witch ought never do.